'Stories – frankly, human stories are always about one thing – death. The inevitability of death.'

J.R.R. TOLKIEN
in a 1968 BBC interview

DOOMED TO DIE

An A–Z of Death in Tolkien

Written and Illustrated by
TOM RACINE

WILLIAM MORROW
An Imprint of HarperCollins*Publishers*

HarperCollins*Publishers*
195 Broadway
New York, NY 10007

www.tolkien.co.uk
www.tolkienestate.com

Published by HarperCollins*Publishers* 2025
1

Library of Congress Cataloging-in-Publication Data
has been applied for.

ISBN 978-0-06-347442-0

Printed and bound in Latvia by PNB.

To the Professor, for endless inspiration.

To Tolkien fans, for your passion.

To Katie and Sam, for the joy and love you bring.

And to Kim, my Lúthien of 35 years and forevermore.

DOOMED TO DIE

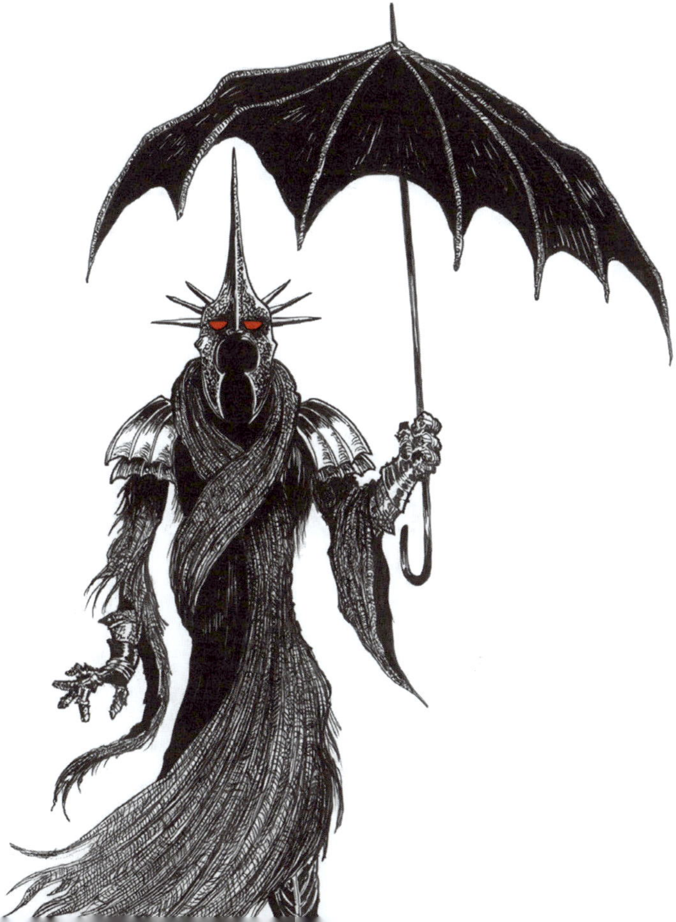

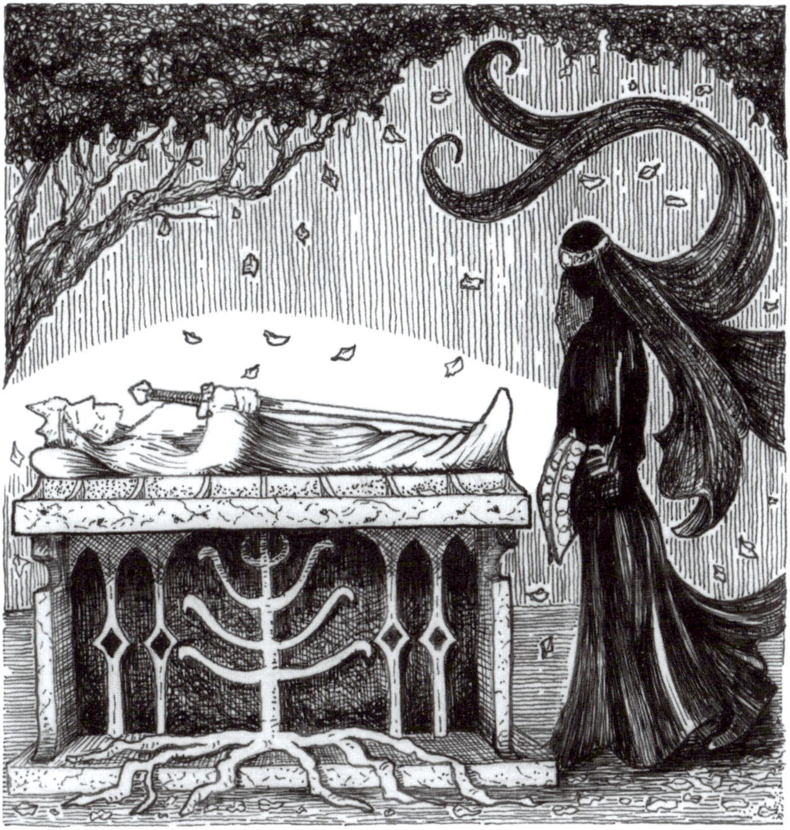

A is for ARWEN broken by sorrows

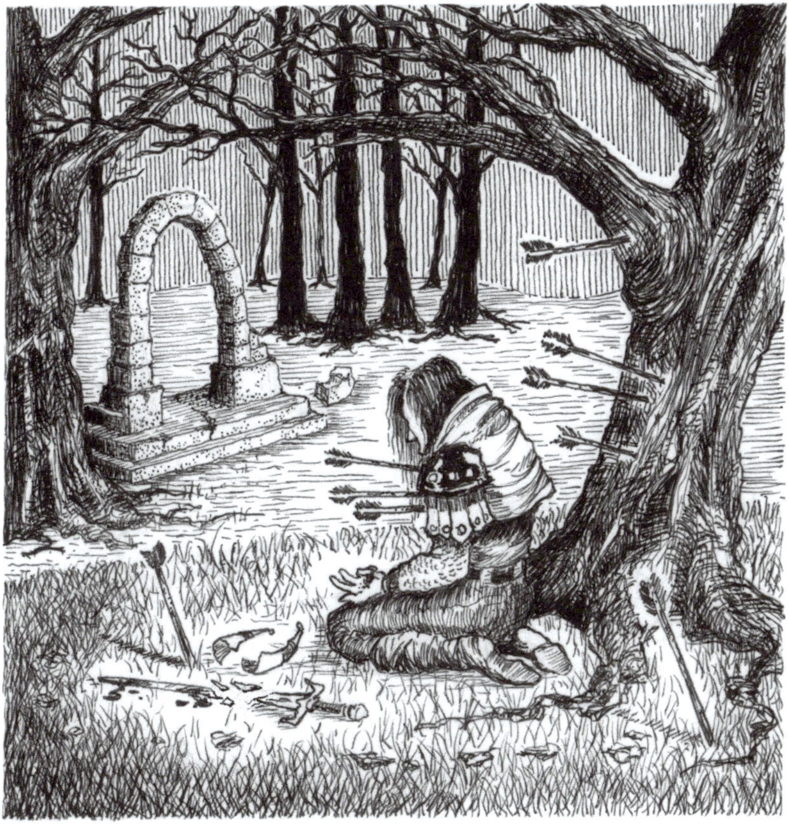

B is for Boromir punctured by arrows

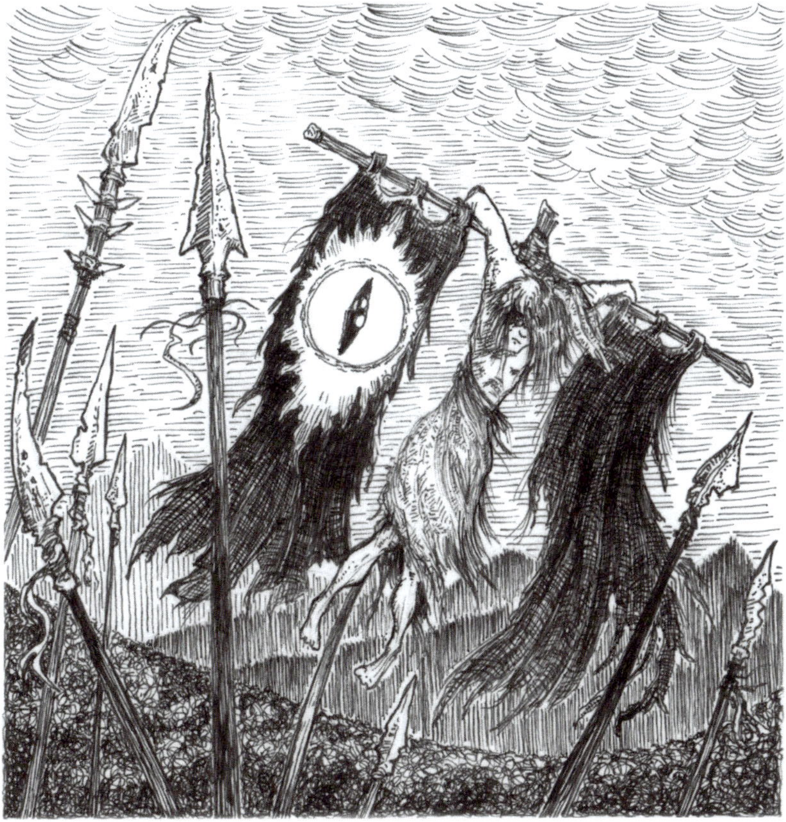

C is for CELEBRIMBOR hung out to dry

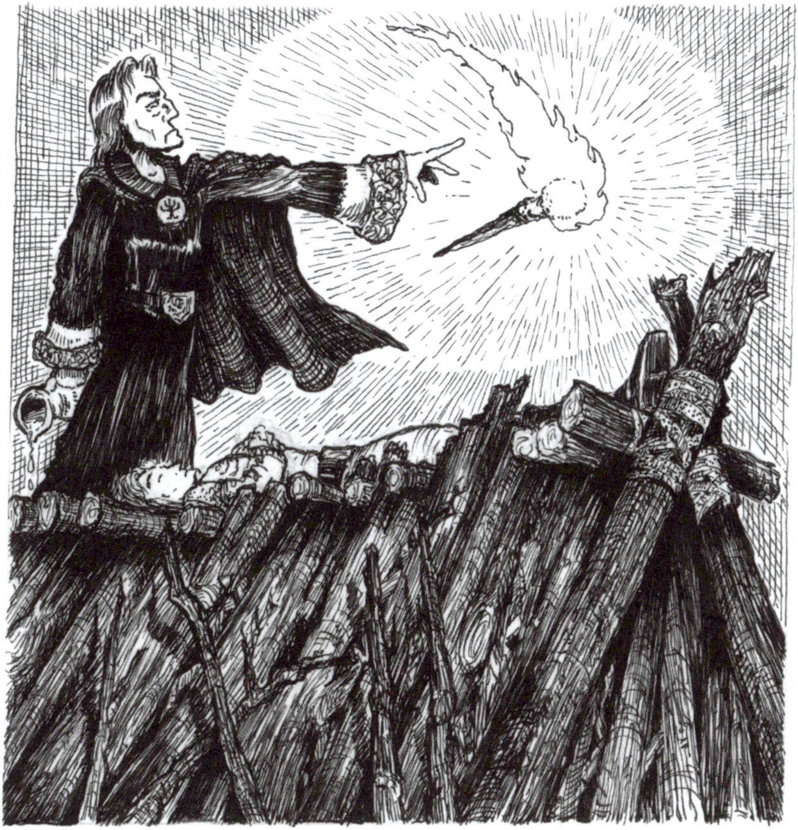

D is for DENETHOR who elected to fry

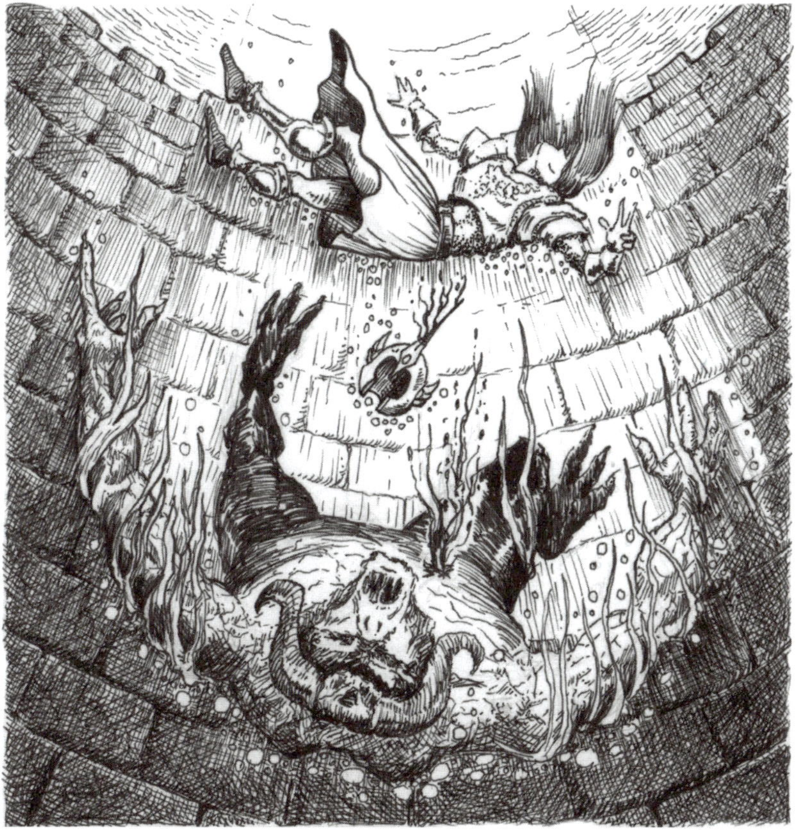

E is for ECTHELION drowned in a fountain

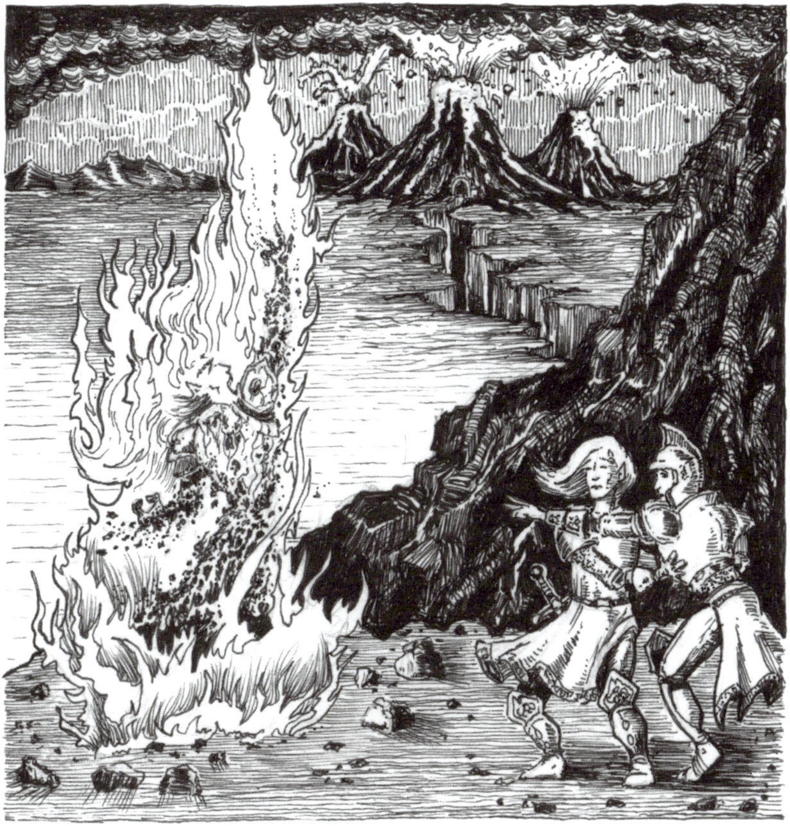

F is for FËANOR burned to ash on a mountain

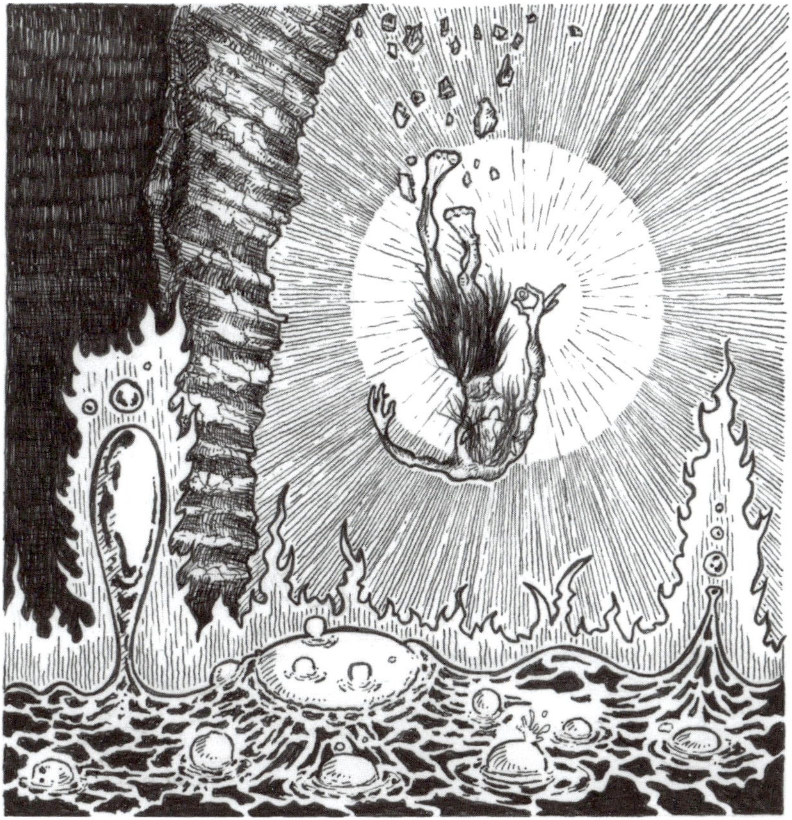

G is for GOLLUM doomed for failure

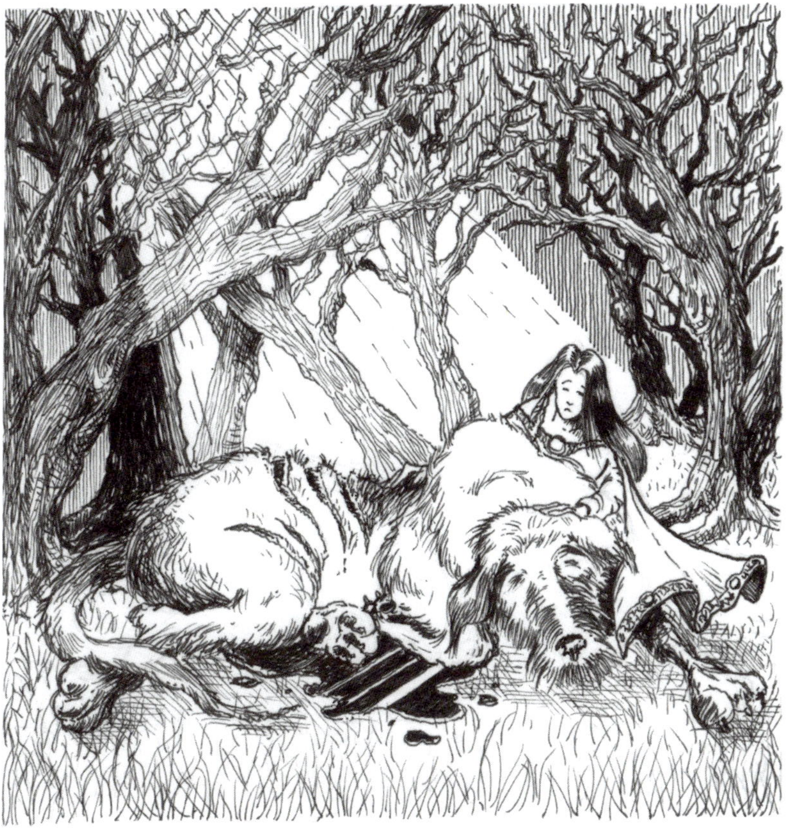

H is for HUAN, Lúthien's saviour

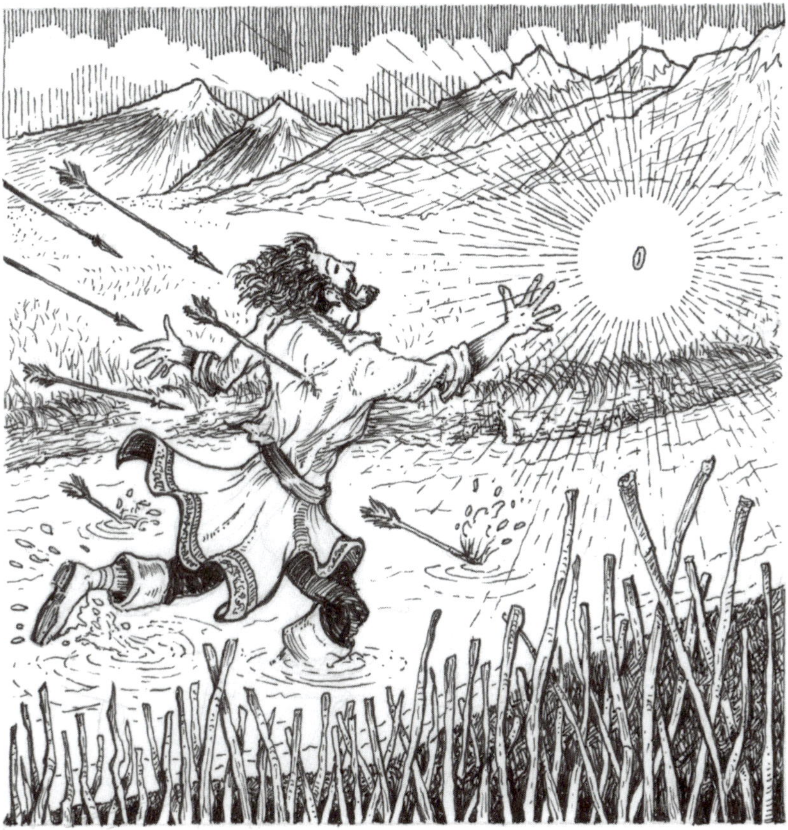

I is for ISILDUR betrayed by the Ring

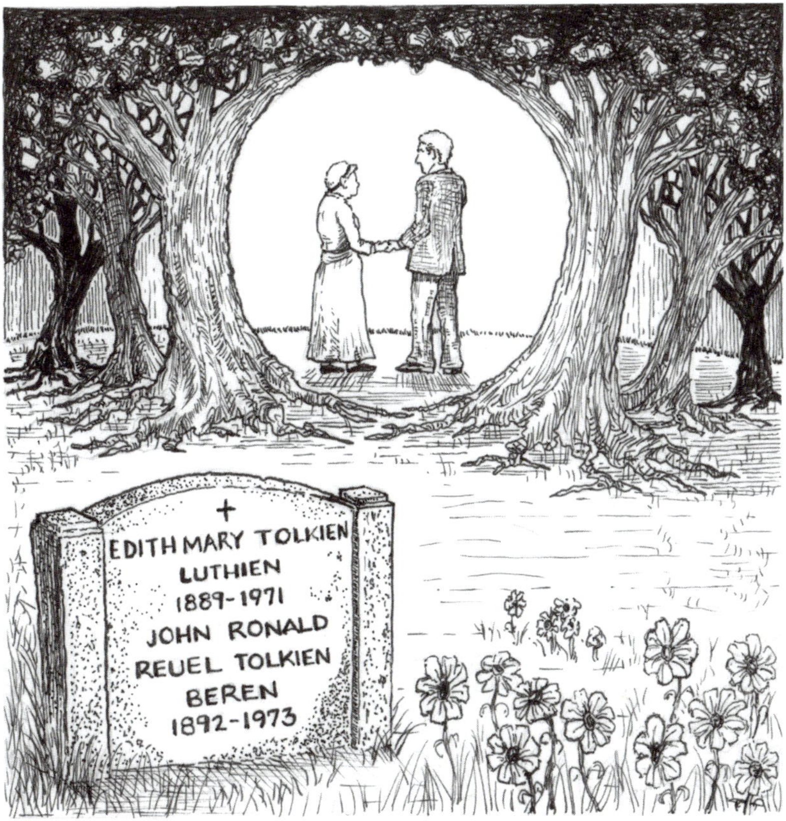
+
EDITH MARY TOLKIEN
LUTHIEN
1889-1971
JOHN RONALD
REUEL TOLKIEN
BEREN
1892-1973

J is for J.R.R. to whom we owe everything

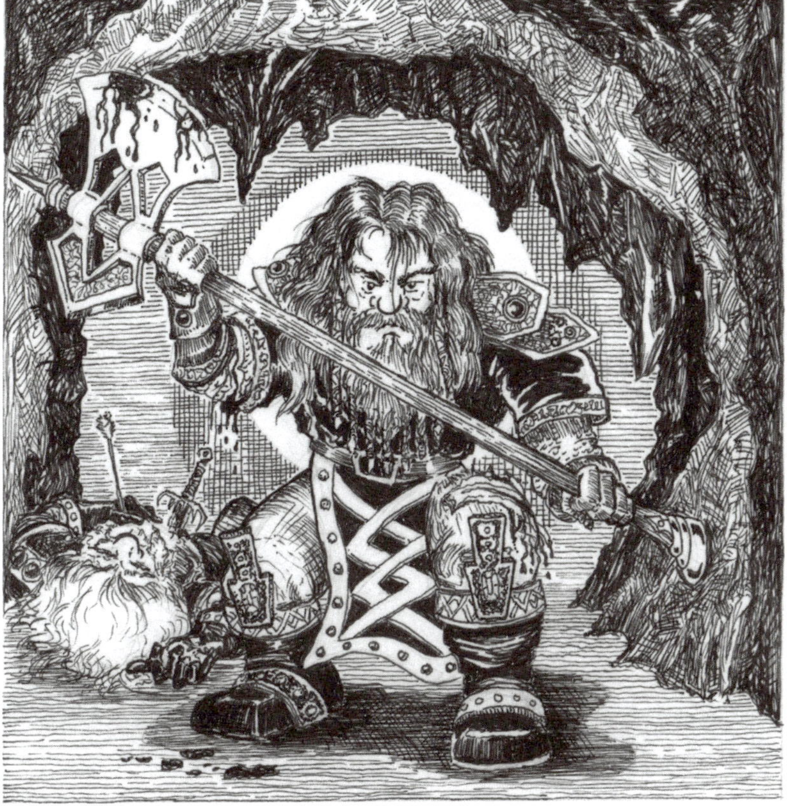

K is for KILI who defended most grimly

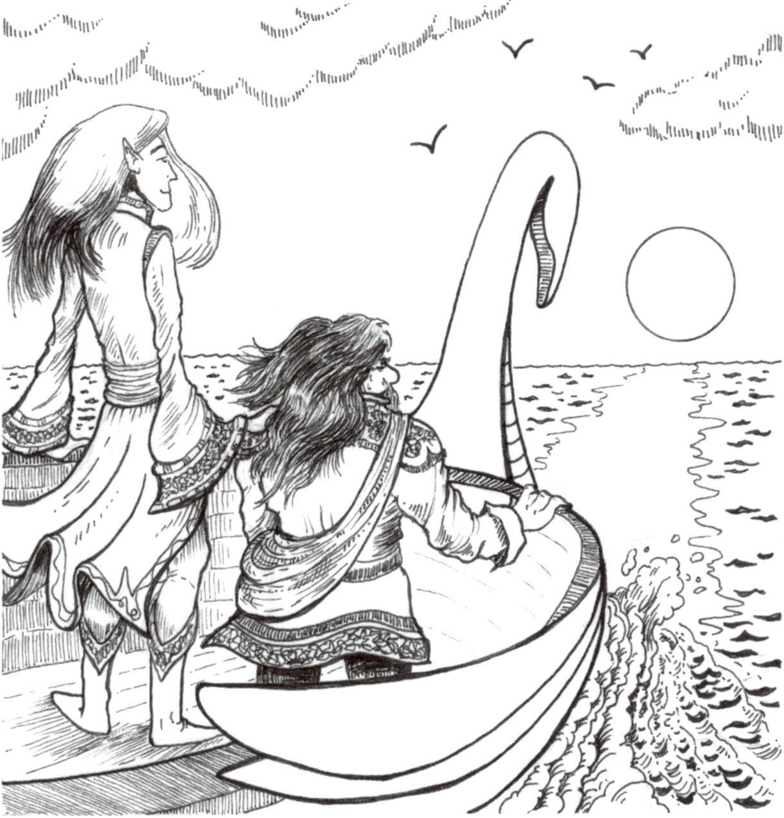

L is for LEGOLAS, undying with Gimli

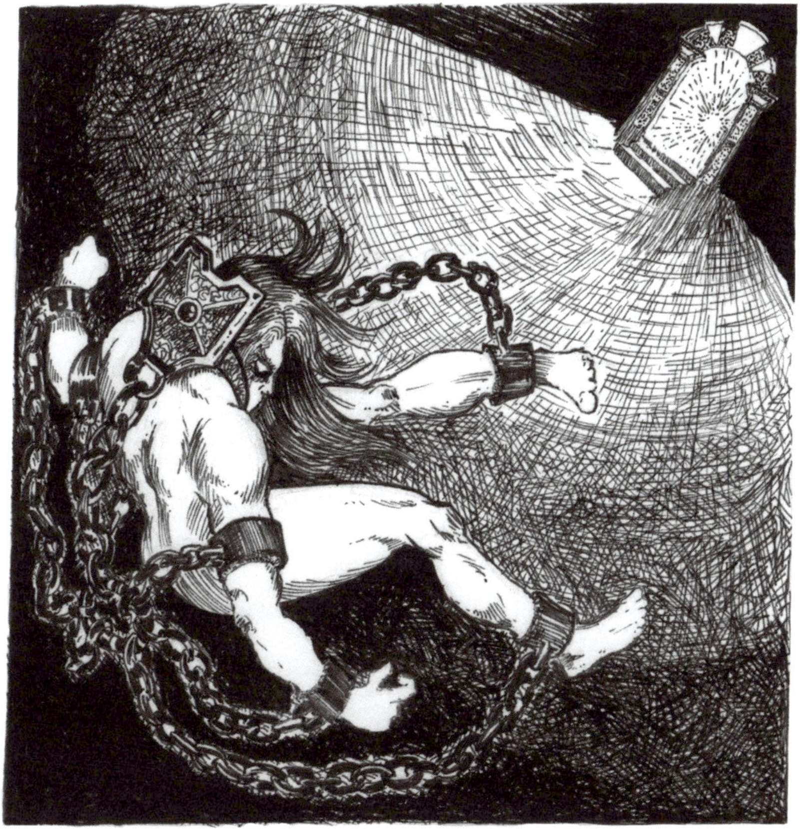

M is for Morgoth shackled in a chain

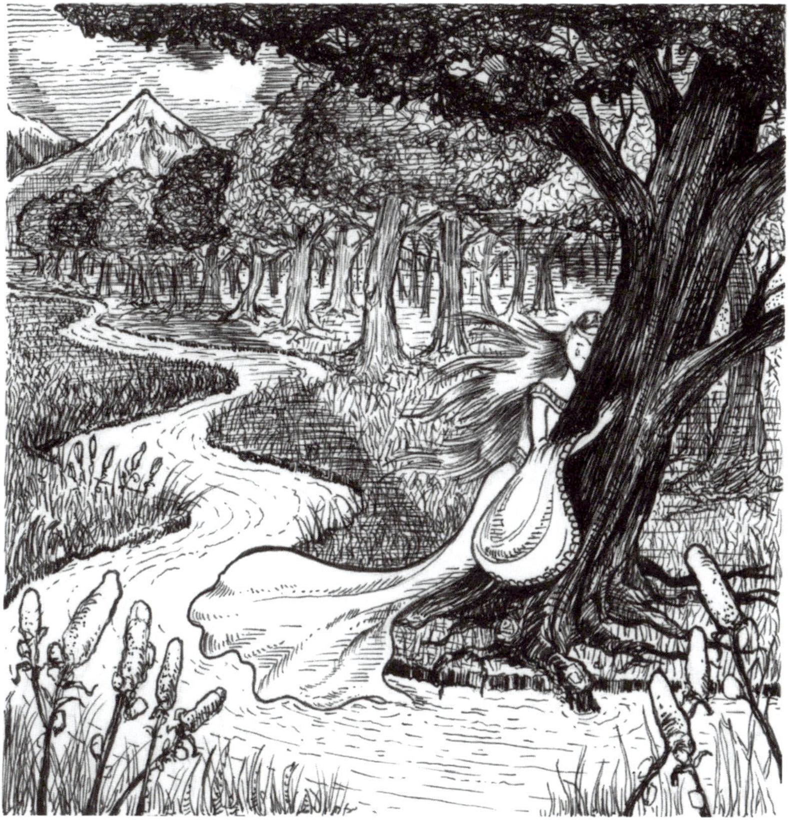

N is for NIMRODEL, tears flowing like rain

.

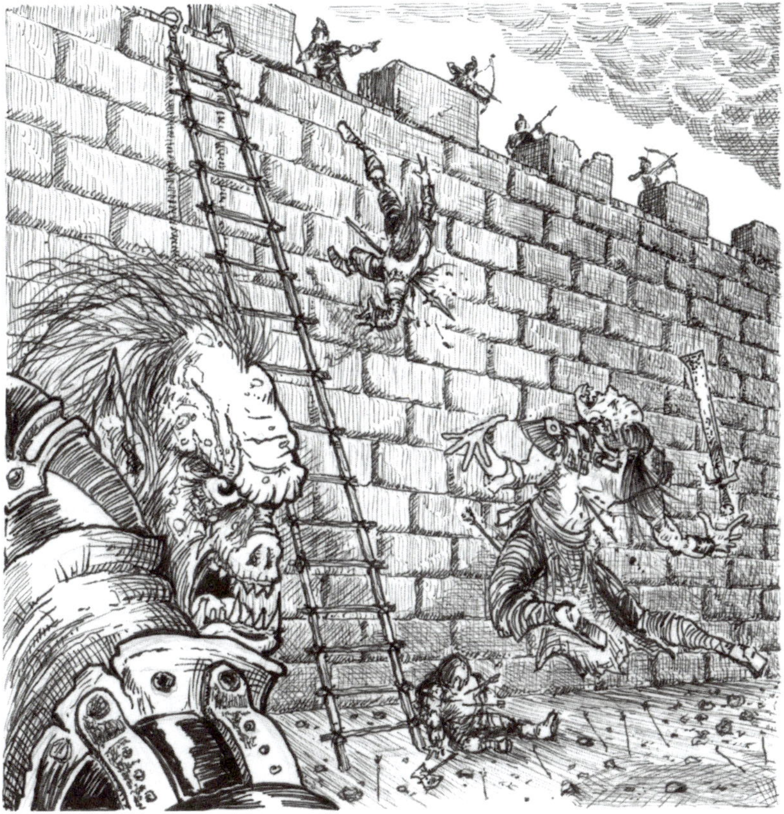

O is for ORCS twisted to evil ends

P is for Pippin buried with friends

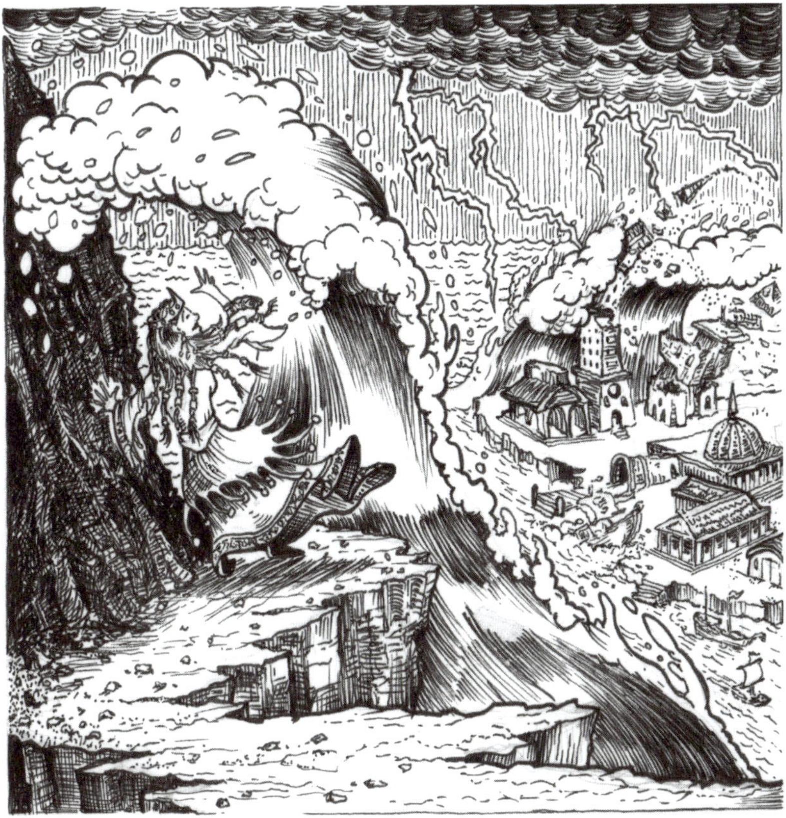

Q is for Queen Tar-Míriel in Númenor drowned

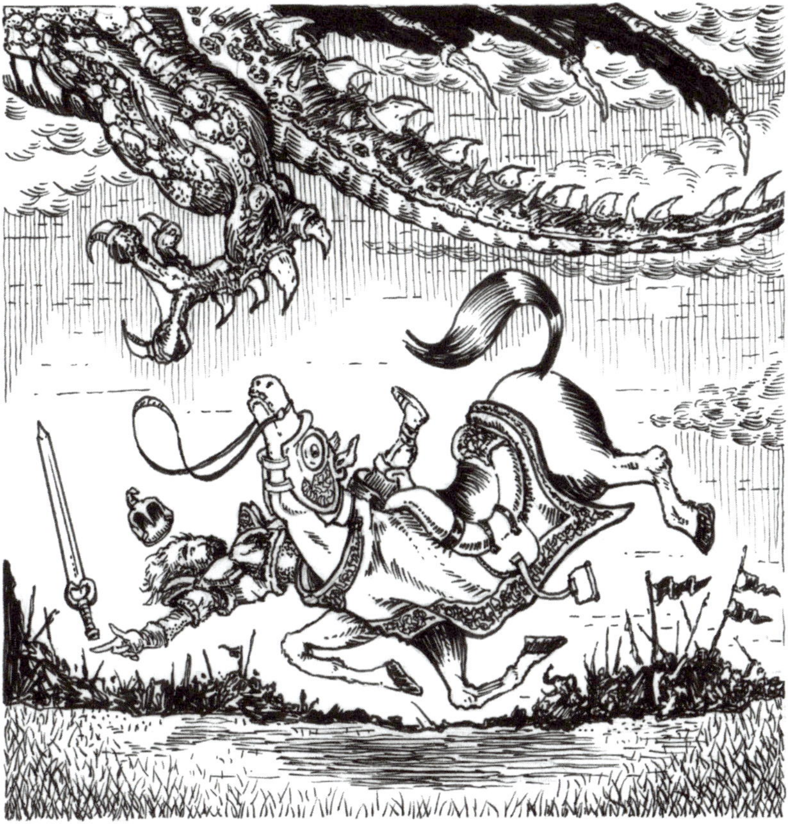

R is for Rohan's King Théoden downed

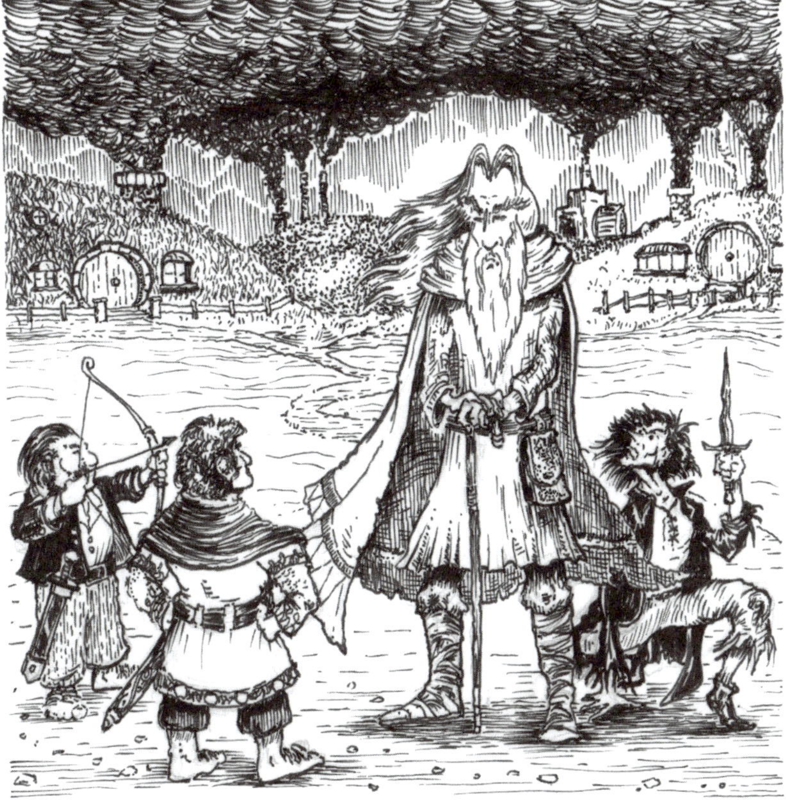

S is for SARUMAN by Wormtongue betrayed

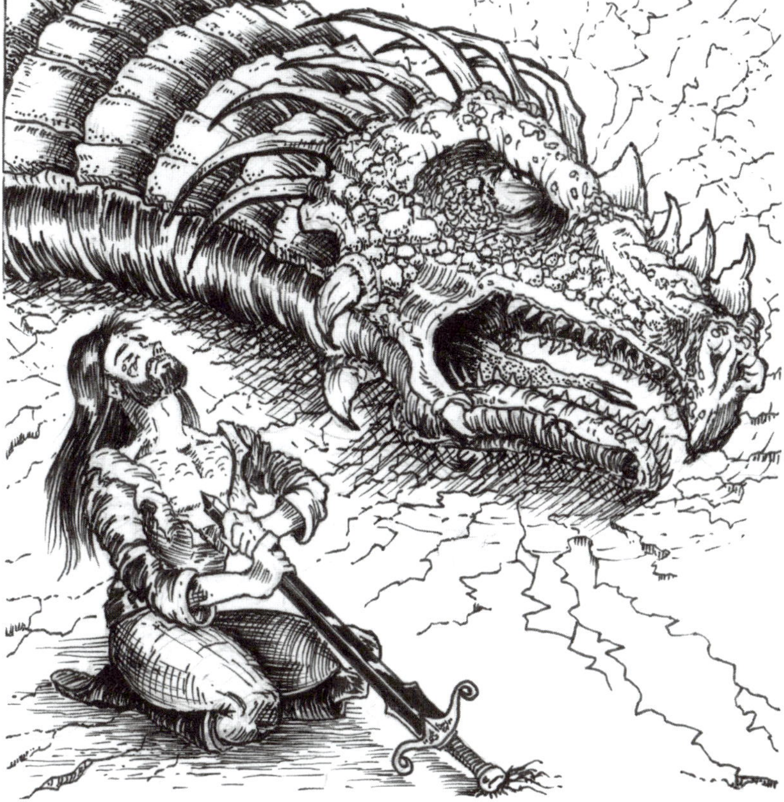

T is for Túrin impaled on a blade

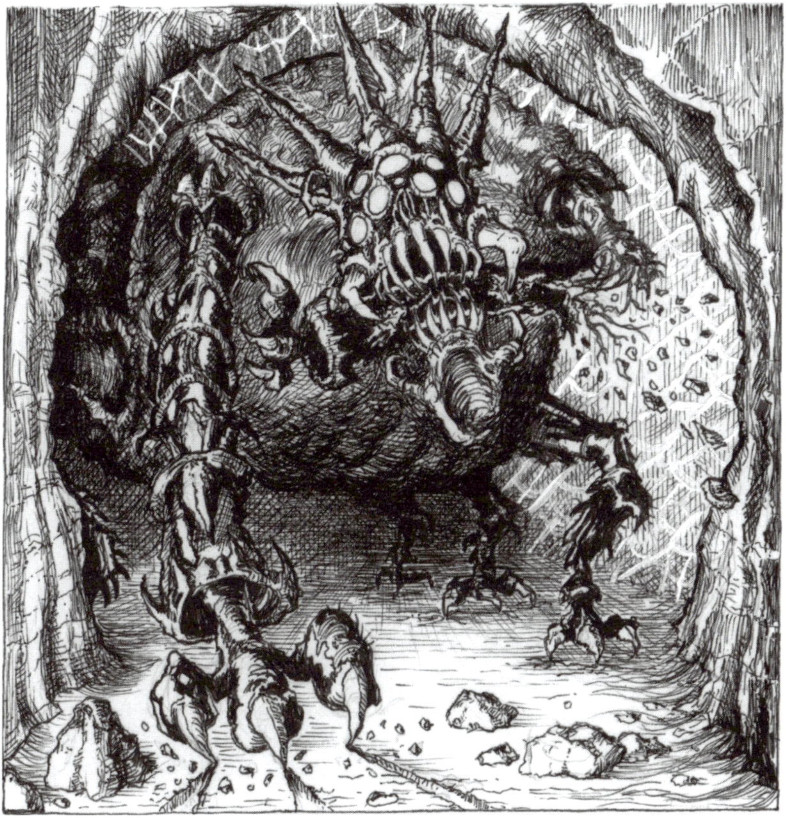

U is for UNGOLIANT whose last meal was gory

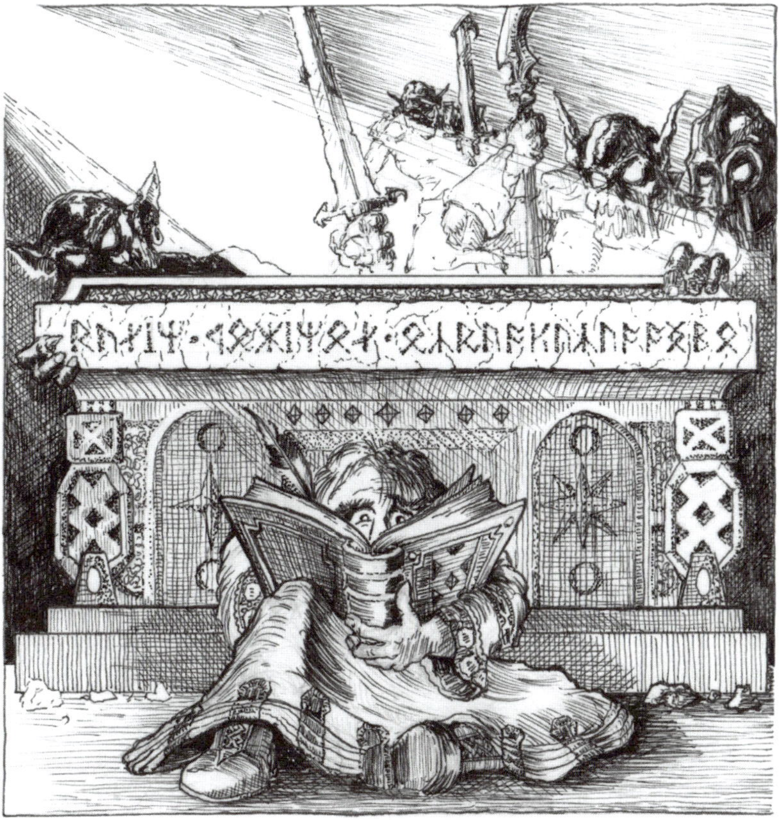

V is for the VALIANT "They are coming!" by ORI

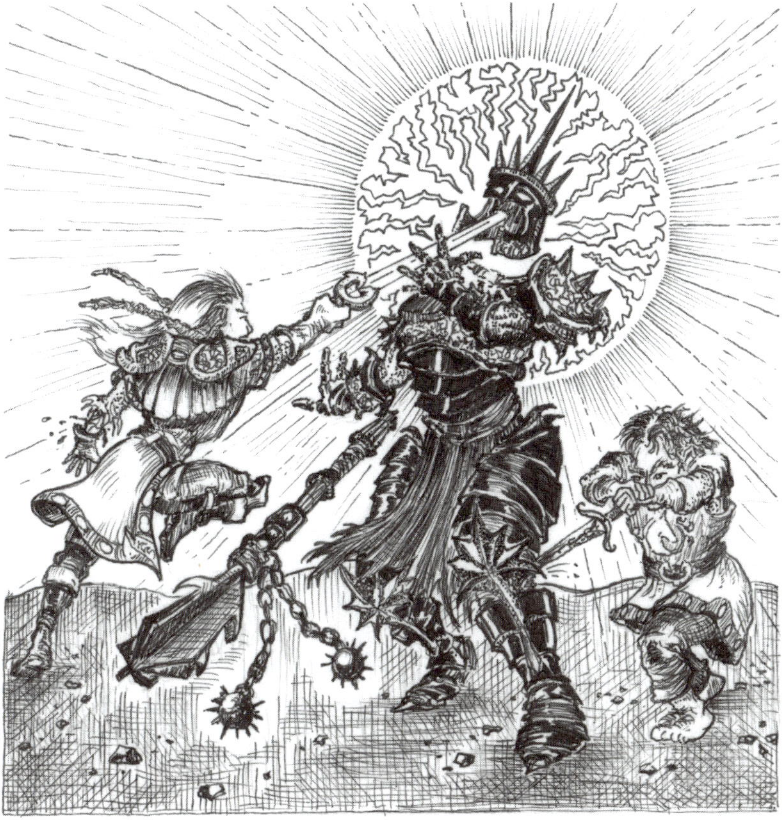

W is for **WITCH-KING**, his head run through

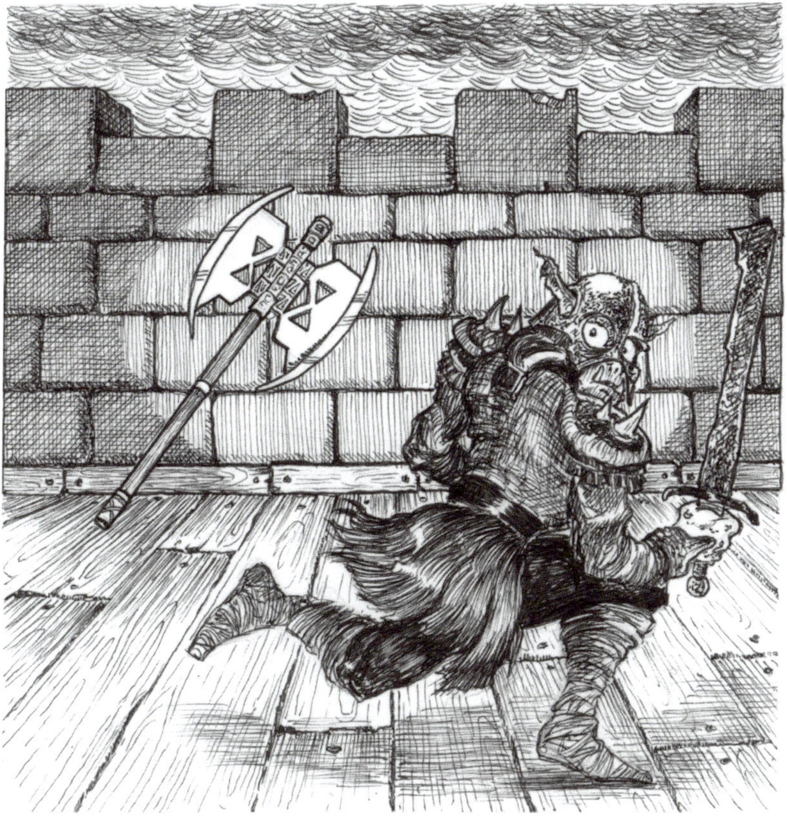

X is for AXE; Gimli's killed forty-two

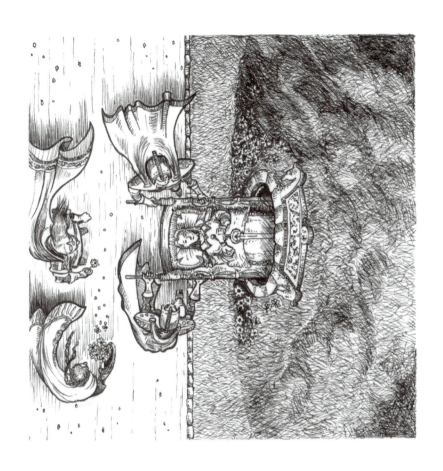

Y is for YOUNG Théodred slain in a fight

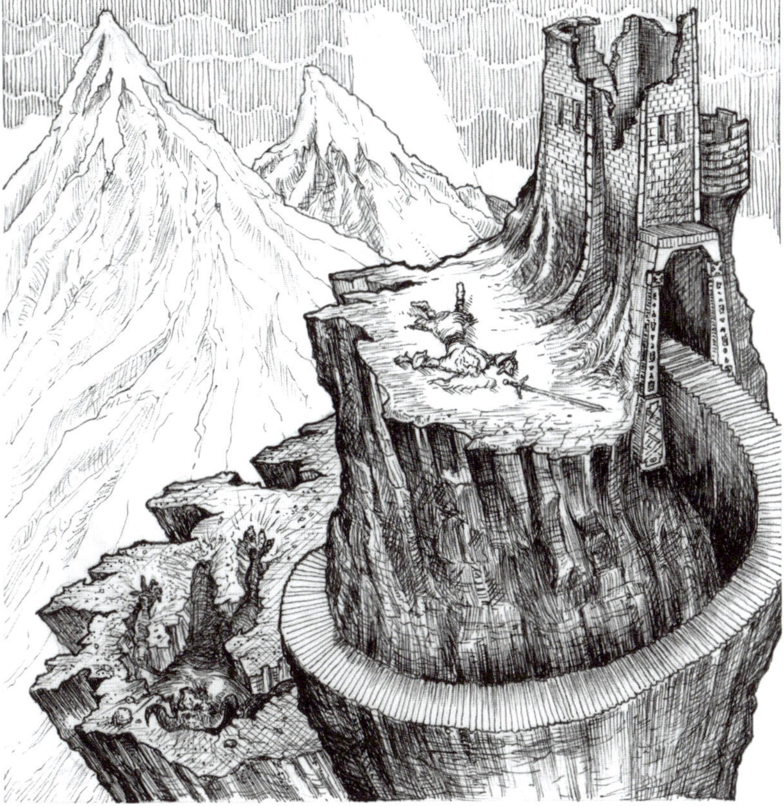

Z is for ZIRAKZIGIL where Gandalf turned white

APPENDICES OF DOOM

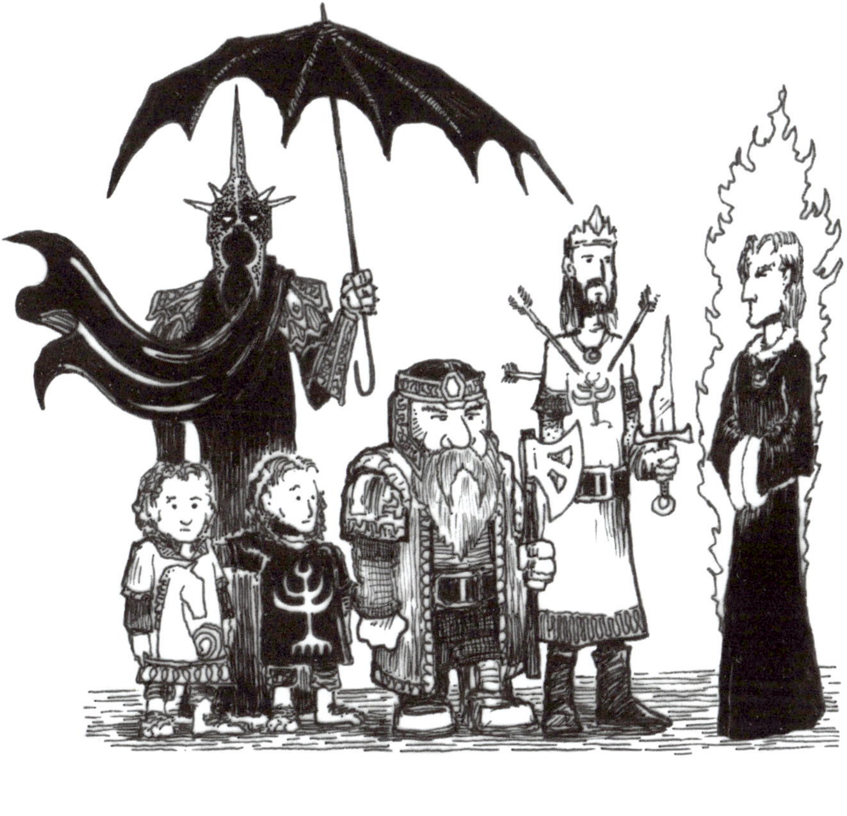

INSPIRATION

The inspiration for *Doomed to Die* comes not only from my deep love and respect for Professor J.R.R. Tolkien, but also an artist I have been inspired by my entire life, Edward Gorey. Specifically, his most well-known work, the fantastic *The Gashlycrumb Tinies*.

I discovered the *Tinies* and Gorey's work in my teens as an aspiring comic book artist and cartoonist. I'm endlessly fascinated by the process of illustration, and forty years on I still feel like I'm learning something every time I draw. I don't claim to be anywhere remotely near the level of a genius that Gorey was, but pen and ink has woven its way through my entire artistic career. I have always adored the skritching sound of a nib pen on Bristol board and the feel of a brush or a felt tip as they glide over the surface.

Every year I like to participate in the online Inktober challenge. It's a nice excuse for doing some traditional drawing, as most of my professional work is now done digitally for graphic design and video creation. Sometimes you just want to feel the surface of the paper and enjoy getting your hands dirty. My first Inktober post is always inspired by Gorey, with some sort of *Gashlycrumb* homage. This year I was persuaded to jump in mostly by my two kids, who often participate with their own drawings and who love to see what I have in my sketchbook.

I had recently started diving more into social media, and discovered that Tolkien fandom is deep and vast. I was humbled and thrilled to discover

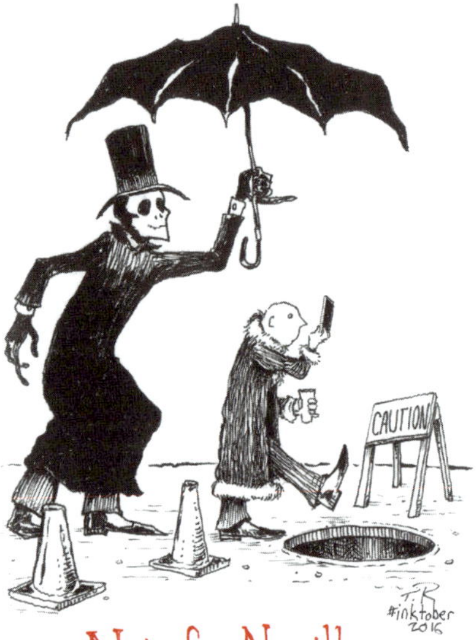
CAUTION
#inktober
2016

N is for Neville,
done in by his phone.

people who knew so much more of Tolkien's lore than I did, many of whom were so much younger than me! For years I was King of the Nerds and Keeper of Obscure Trivia in my friend group, but when you really start digging into almost any serious fandom, you realize that there are higher levels of Nerd that rule them all!

All these wonderful Tolkien folks re-ignited my lifelong love of the Professor's legendarium. Granted, it was never far from my mind; I'm a huge fan of Peter Jackson's films, and my shelves have many a copy of *The Hobbit*, *The Lord of the Rings*, *The Silmarillion*, *The Children of Húrin* and more, but I confess it had been a number of years since I read any of them. I started doing a little comic about the Blue Wizards for my own amusement, with no intention of trying to build an audience or make money from the art. I was drawing for drawing's sake, and was truly enjoying the creative process.

PREPARATION

So it was in late September 2024 I decided I would draw a few Inktobers and started to consider what this year's Gorey homage would be. At once, the beautiful image of Arwen, dressed all in black and standing at the foot of Aragorn's tomb, came into my mind. The words *'A is for Arwen, done in by sorrow'* followed immediately.

For B, Boromir was obvious. He has always been a favourite character of mine, and the death scene Tolkien wrote for him is unbelievably powerful. *'B is for Boromir, pierced by many an arrow.'* It rhymed!

I knew I was on to something, and within an hour I had the whole thing planned out. I looked at my copy of *Amphigorey* and measured the *Gashlycrumb* images, determined to do my best to bring my interpretation of Gorey's work to life using Tolkien characters.

I posted *'A is for Arwen'* on Instagram on October 1st and was pleasantly surprised to get over 100 likes and many comments about how much fun this was. As I posted more letters over the next few days, I started noticing likes from people I didn't know, and they began sharing them quite a bit. My engagement with social media has created barely a ripple over the years, so this was really quite enjoyable.

Then, after the letter J, I decided to make an Instagram reel of the first ten letters. It's a simple slideshow and easy to do, and by that afternoon it had clocked up 3,000 views. I put my phone away and went about my day with a little more spring in my step.

That night, the number was 15,000. The next morning, 30,000. That evening, 70,000, and next day, 125,000. Eventually, more than 400,000 people had watched it. Later reels did equally well, and with a daily influx of comments like *'Where can I buy this?'* I began to think that perhaps I should get permission to do a book.

CELEBRATION

It's one thing to put some fan art on Instagram, but it's quite another to get it published and sold. There are rules, and copyright cannot be ignored. I knew that HarperCollins was the only publisher authorized by the Tolkien Estate, so I sent an email on a wing and a prayer to their office in New York.

To my amazement I heard back from David Brawn, publisher of literary estates at HarperCollins UK. He wrote me an email, the first two sentences of which were the most amazing rollercoaster of emotions I've ever experienced in electronic form. Basically, *'I absolutely love this idea'* (be still, my heart!) followed by *'There is no way this can be published'* (be crushed, my heart!)

To hear that the person who has published pretty much everything we've seen of Tolkien's work over the last thirty years thought what I did was great was one of the high points of my artistic life. David, however, wanted to pitch it to the Estate, because he saw the potential of it, although he cautioned me not to get my hopes up because no one had never done a Tolkien book like this before.

In the sports world, they say *'THAT is why they play the games.'* Less than a year later, and beyond my wildest dreams, this book exists.

ASPIRATION

I have only two hopes for *Doomed to Die*. First, that you enjoy it. That in the grim spirit of Tolkien and Gorey, two of the great creators of the twentieth century, you smile, chuckle, or are moved by some of the many deaths that occur in the pages of the Professor's work.

And secondly, that it inspires you to read or re-read *The Hobbit* or *The Lord of the Rings* or *The Silmarillion* or *Unfinished Tales*, or any of the other books on Tolkien's very long list, or to finally dive deeper into the legendarium like you've wanted to all your life. As the steps on the road to this, I have provided what I hope will be some helpful notes at the back of this book.

If you haven't read any of the books, or if your only exposure to Tolkien is through the live-action movies, the old animations or the recent *Rings of Power* series, I urge you to go to the original sources and explore their pages. Oh, the journey that awaits you!

Most Middle-earth fans really just want to be Hobbits; to curl up with a good book and think about what we're having for second breakfast, elevenses, luncheon, afternoon tea, dinner and supper. And to immerse ourselves in a world filled with Elves, Dwarves, Ents, Wizards and Dark Lords. And, of course . . . Death.

TOM RACINE
Astron the 25th, in the year 2025
of the Seventh Age (by Shire Reckoning)

ARWEN UNDÓMIEL daughter of Elrond, Lord of the Elves of Rivendell, chose to lead a mortal life because of her love of Aragorn, who eventually became King of the Reunited Kingdom of Arnor and Gondor.

She decided not to sail into the West with her Father and the rest of her people, and gifted her passage to the Undying Lands to Frodo, the Ringbearer, so that, if he wished, he might journey there to fully recover from his heroic ordeal.

Arwen ruled by Aragorn's side for 120 years until his death at age 210. She decided to leave Minas Tirith at that time, and journeyed to Lothlórien, now abandoned because the Elves had all departed Middle-earth for good. A year after her beloved's passing, she gave up her life in the year 121 of the Fourth Age, and was buried upon the hill of Cerin Amroth, in the heart of what remained of Lothlórien. Thus ended one of the great love stories in all of Tolkien's books.

— *The Lord of the Rings*, Appendix A

BOROMIR, son of Denethor II, perished on the slopes of Parth Galen, defending the Hobbits Merry and Pippin from a horde of Uruk-hai, Great Orcs sent by the wizard Saruman to try and capture the Ring. Boromir's deep love of Gondor and his desire to save his people from the overwhelming threat of Sauron caused him to try and take the Ring from Frodo in a fit of madness.

The Ring's insidious power had been working on Boromir's fears for many weeks, and in a moment of weakness, he was taken by its power. Upon Frodo's escape, Boromir realized to his great shame what he had done.

Almost immediately, the Uruk-hai attacked, and Boromir was sent to find Merry and Pippin who had run off in search of their friend Frodo. He saved them initially by slaying dozens of Orcs, but their numbers proved too great and pierced by many arrows, Boromir's life was ended.

— *The Two Towers*, 'The Departure of Boromir'

CELEBRIMBOR's work as a master craftsman looms large over the history of Middle-earth. His grandfather was the legendary Fëanor, creator of the Silmarils, three gems that captured the unsullied light of the Two Trees of Valinor, land of the Valar.

Celebrimbor's forging of the Great Rings of Power would shape the fates of the Second and Third Ages. He desired greatly to achieve the craftsmanship and fame of his grandfather, and after befriending the great Dwarven smith Narvi and learning about the magical metal *mithril*, Celebrimbor devised the moon-runes upon the Doors of Durin at the West-gate of Moria.

However, he was then influenced and deceived by Sauron as they together forged the Rings of Power, who was then in his fair guise as Annatar, the Lord of Gifts. Unbeknownst to Celebrimbor, merely by being involved in their creation, Sauron had tainted the Nine Rings for Men, and the Seven Rings for Dwarves. After Sauron returned to Mordor, Celebrimbor alone forged the three Elven-rings. And of course, Sauron then used his magic and his malice to forge the One Ring to rule them all in secret.

Sauron later attacked Eregion, capturing Celebrimbor and torturing him to discover the location of the Nine and the Seven, but Celebrimbor would not reveal the Three. When Celebrimbor died, Sauron hung his body on a pole and displayed him like a banner in front of his armies.

— *Unfinished Tales*, 'The History of Galadriel and Celeborn'

DENETHOR II was the last of the line of the Stewards of Gondor. For nearly a thousand years, the Stewards ruled Gondor from the city of Minas Tirith after the last King of Gondor, Eärnur, died in the year 2050 of the Third Age, leaving no heirs.

Denethor ruled during the rise of Sauron in neighbouring Mordor. The father of Boromir and Faramir, Denethor was a wise and strong leader, but after much tragedy in his life, and seeking more knowledge to protect his people from the growing menace of Sauron so near his borders, he started using a *palantír* to gain information and insight into the Enemy's mind.

Though a man of great willpower and intelligence, Denethor was slowly corrupted by what the *palantír* showed him through his dealings with both Sauron and Saruman.

Towards the end of the war against Sauron, he saw what he thought was the end of all things, and he built a pyre to burn himself and his badly wounded son, Faramir, exclaiming 'Better to burn sooner than late, for burn we must!'

— The Return of the King, 'The Siege of Gondor'

ECTHELION was the leader of the People of the Fountain in the hidden Elven city of Gondolin. He was renowned as both a warrior and the greatest singer and musician of all the people there.

Gondolin remained hidden for nearly 400 years, until its location was betrayed by Maeglin, the nephew of King Turgon, its founder. Morgoth had long sought Gondolin and now he set a great army of Orcs and Balrogs on the city. Ecthelion and his people slew more Orcs than had ever been slain, as well as three Balrogs, but he was wounded in battle and was carried away to the great Fountain of the King.

There, Ecthelion faced off with Gothmog, Lord of Balrogs. Ecthelion took many wounds, especially to his hand and he lost his sword. Gothmog raised his whip to deliver the final blow, but Ecthelion leapt at his foe and drove the tall spike of his helmet into the chest of Gothmog, and entwining their legs, Ecthelion pushed Gothmog into the deep fountain, where they both died. Truly one of the greatest of all Elven heroes.

— *The Silmarillion*, 'Of Tuor and the Fall of Gondolin'

FËANOR, greatest of the Noldor Elves, created the three Silmarils, gems of surpassing beauty that literally captured the light of the Two Trees of Valinor. Fëanor's masterpieces drive all the tragic deeds that are recounted in *The Silmarillion*, and his grandson Celebrimbor was nearly his equal in craftsmanship.

After Morgoth stole the Silmarils, Fëanor and his sons swore the Oath of Fëanor, which would lead to kin-slayings, ship burnings, betrayals and death for years to come. Eventually, Fëanor confronted Morgoth at his fortress of Angband, but he and his sons were ambushed by Balrogs, and Fëanor was mortally wounded and he died. But his spirit was so fiery, so full of rage and passion, that it reduced his body to ashes, the only person to die this way in all of the legendarium.

— *The Silmarillion*, 'Of the Return of the Noldor'

GOLLUM's long, sad life, twisted and controlled by the One Ring, ends at least in a brief moment of triumph, as he bites the Ring off Frodo's finger inside Mount Doom. Seventy-eight years after that filthy Hobbit Baggins stole it from him, his precious birthday present was back in his grasp. Until, of course, he loses his balance on the edge of the Cracks of Doom and falls into the lava, destroying both the Ring and Sauron.

The themes of death, grief, and pity are central to all of Tolkien's works, and Gollum may be the greatest example of that. Gandalf notes that 'My heart tells me that he has some part to play yet, for good or ill, before the end; and when that comes, the pity of Bilbo may rule the fate of many – yours not least.' Gollum's path is a sad and tragic one, but there's a strange comfort knowing that in his last moments, he was reunited with his Precious.

— The Hobbit **and** *The Lord of the Rings*

HUAN, the Hound of Valinor, is many people's favourite beast in all of Tolkien. A wolfhound the size of a small horse, Huan was a hunting dog of Oromë, one of the most powerful of the Valar. Huan was immortal, tireless, and was gifted the ability to speak three times before he died.

The full story of Huan is too long to recap here, but he is eventually entwined in the great love story of Beren and Lúthien, befriending them and taking pity upon their plight. In Beren's great quest of retrieving a Silmaril, his hand was bitten off by the monstrous werewolf, Carcharoth, and driven mad by the Silmaril now in its belly, Carcharoth went mad. A group of hunters including Huan managed to kill the great werewolf, but Huan was mortally wounded. His loyalty and protection of Beren and Lúthien is legendary and his passing is one of the most emotional scenes in their story.

— *The Silmarillion*, 'Of Beren and Lúthien'

ISILDUR, son of Elendil, the first High King of Gondor, is most famous for being the one who cuts the One Ring off of Sauron's hand, later losing it in the River Anduin after being ambushed by Orcs. Isildur tragically ignored the advice of both Elrond and Círdan the Shipwright, who urged him to destroy the Ring right then and there, instead desiring to keep it as weregild (tribute payment) for the deaths of his father and brother.

However, about two years after the fall of Sauron, Isildur and his men were ambushed by a huge army of Orcs, and three of his sons died in the fighting. Isildur was urged by his eldest son Elendur to flee with the Ring. He did so reluctantly, slipping the Ring on his finger and, being invisible, thought he could escape the Orcs. But the Ring betrayed Isildur, slipping from his finger, and he was slain by many arrows.

— Unfinished Tales, 'The Disaster of the Gladden Fields'

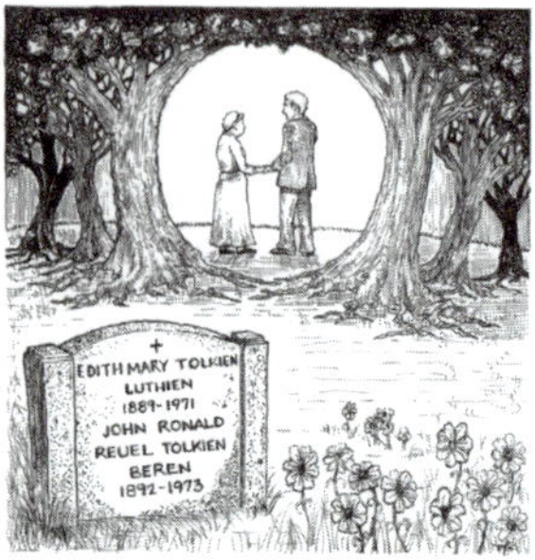

EDITH MARY TOLKIEN
LUTHIEN
1889-1971
JOHN RONALD
REUEL TOLKIEN
BEREN
1892-1973

J.R.R. TOLKIEN based the characters of Beren and Lúthien on himself and his beloved wife, Edith. After Beren's death while retrieving the Silmaril from the great werewolf Carcharoth, Lúthien soon wasted away from grief. Their spirits found their way to the Halls of Mandos in the West, home of the Valar, and there Lúthien sang a song of grief and love that moved the heart of Mandos to pity, a thing that had never happened. After Mandos sought counsel, Lúthien was offered a unique choice of eternal life in bliss with the Valar, or to return to Middle-earth with Beren and lead a mortal life. She chose mortality with the man she loved.

In Professor Tolkien's own life, however, it was his wife who passed first in 1971. He wrote to his son Christopher the following words of surpassing beauty and grief: 'I never called Edith *Lúthien*, but she was the source of the story that in time became the chief part of the *Silmarillion*. . . . In those days, her hair was raven, her skin clear, her eyes brighter than you have ever seen them, and she could sing—and *dance*. But the story has gone crooked, & I am left, and *I* cannot plead before the inexorable Mandos.' In that letter, he proposed the inscription on the gravestone to be 'Edith Mary Tolkien. 1889–1971. Lúthien.'

— The Letters of J.R.R. Tolkien

KILI was one of the thirteen dwarves who went on a quest with the Hobbit, Bilbo Baggins, and Gandalf the Wizard to reclaim their ancestral land of Erebor, many years after it had been taken by Smaug the Dragon. Kili and his brother Fili were nephews of the great Thorin Oakenshield, and were by far the youngest of the Dwarves in that tale. As such, they were often described as much more exuberant than their companions, and they were inseparable from one another.

Sadly, Thorin, now King Under the Mountain, was mortally wounded in the Battle of the Five Armies, and Kili and his brother were slain bravely protecting their uncle from the Goblins. They were buried with Thorin with great honour, ending the line of Dwarven Kings descended from Thrór.

— *The Hobbit*, 'The Return Journey'

LEGOLAS and Gimli form a friendship that I believe to be the best in Tolkien's lore. Often the mistrust or outright hatred between the Elves and Dwarves comes up throughout the many stories, and even in *The Lord of the Rings* when they meet, Legolas and Gimli have no love for one another, and even clash outside the Mines of Moria's Doors of Durin about which race was at fault for the friendship of old's failure. But when Gimli enters Lothlórien and meets the Lady Galadriel, all that changes.

I believe that when you read the Appendices and hear about these two friends' further journeys and friendship, it strikes at the core of why we love Tolkien's writings. Overcoming differences, not being tied to the past, appreciating different worlds and cultures, and finding people to share a love of travel and adventure.

Their playful competition to see who can kill more Orcs is a highlight of the books, and in the Appendices we learn that they went on many adventures after the Great Quest of the Ring was ended. They would help rebuild Minas Tirith, and spend time in Rohan in the Glittering Caves. In the end, after Aragorn passed, Legolas built a grey ship, and taking a now aged Gimil with him, sailed into the West to join his people. Gimli became the first and only Dwarf to see the beauty of Valinor.

— *The Lord of the Rings*, Appendix B, 'Later Events Concerning the Members of the Fellowship of the Ring'

MORGOTH, or Melkor as he was originally known, was the mightiest of the Ainur, the first beings created by Ilúvatar. As they all sang in harmony to create the world, Melkor sang in discordance with them, wanting to make his own music. He is the chief adversary in *The Silmarillion*, causing much destruction and pain for thousands of years.

It's not quite accurate to say Morgoth 'dies' in any conventional sense, but after many wars and terrible deeds, the Valar finally put him in chains and thrust him through the Door of Night into the Timeless Void, which is outside of time and space, where he could do no more harm. In an unpublished manuscript, Tolkien does write of a prophecy that says Morgoth will return in the Last Battle, but will ultimately be slain by Túrin Turambar, the man he cursed to a life of woe.

— *The Lost Road* 'Part Two: Valinor and Middle-earth'

NIMRODEL, Elf-maiden of Lórien, lived alone in Lothlórien long before the Sindar and Noldor Elves came. And once they did, she feared they would bring nothing but turmoil and destruction to her beloved lands. She wasn't wrong.

She did see the good in one Sindar Elf: King Amroth of the Wood. Though she loved him, she would not marry him. Then in the Third Age, the Balrog in the Mines of Moria awoke, and she became even more unsettled. Amroth promised to take her south to lands where they could find peace. But on the journey they became separated; Amroth waited for her aboard his ship, but tragically a storm swept this out to sea. He leapt overboard to try to get back to land and his love, but drowned in the attempt.

Nimrodel had settled and was waiting at the River Gilrain, where she fell into a long and deep sleep. When she awoke, she could find no trace of her lover Amroth, and in deep grief, disappears from the stories altogether. All that remains is the river named after her in the foothills of the White Mountains.

— Unfinished Tales, 'The History of Galadriel and Celeborn'

ORCS are soldiers of the armies of Morgoth and Sauron over the many Ages of the world, and they are both loathsome and pitiable. It is said that as far back as the Years of the Trees, Morgoth kidnapped some of the Elves and tortured, twisted, and deformed them into the Orcs. They are an easy thing to hate, as they are almost always portrayed as mindlessly violent and usually in giant armies whose sole purpose is to kill in the name of their cruel masters.

However, their story is deeply tragic in nature. Tolkien wrote, 'And deep in their dark hearts, the Orcs loathed the Master whom they served in fear, the maker only of their misery. This it may be was the vilest deed of Melkor, and the most hateful to Ilúvatar.'

It's hard not to feel a sense of pity and sorrow for the Orcs who never had a choice in what they did, nor could be free from being pawns in the machinations of Morgoth and Sauron.

— *The Silmarillion*, 'Of the Coming of the Elves and the Captivity of Melkor'

PIPPIN (Peregrin Took) and Merry (Meriadoc Brandybuck) were, of course, two of the four Hobbits who were key characters in *The Lord of the Rings*. Upon returning to the Shire, both of them became great leaders. At the end of their lives, they went to Rohan to stay awhile with King Éomer before his death, and then spent the remainder of their time as honoured guests of King Elessar, their old companion Aragorn.

They died around the same time as each other, and were laid to rest in Rath Dínen, where the great Kings and Stewards of Gondor were interred. Some time after, Aragorn succumbed to the Gift of Ilúvatar, and Pippin and Merry were then laid by his side.

— *The Lord of the Rings*, **Appendix B**

QUEEN TAR-MÍRIEL of Númenor truly has one of the more tragic fates, which she most certainly didn't deserve. Her father was King Tar-Palantir, who late in his life tried to restore the old traditions of the Númenóreans, and respect the Elves and the Valar who had always been their allies. But the men of Númenor had long been turning their resentment about their mortality and the Gift of Ilúvatar towards the Elves, and Míriel's cousin, Pharazôn was these men's leader. He forced marriage upon Míriel, and seized the kingship and the Sceptre of Númenor for himself.

In the section of *The Silmarillion* called *Akallabêth*, it is told how Sauron let himself be captured by King Ar-Pharazôn, and commenced poisoning the minds of the king and his people to the point where they created a great fleet, and dared to sail West to wrest from the Valar the secret of immortality. So great was this transgression, that Eru Ilúvatar created a great chasm in the sea, drowning the fleet, and destroying Númenor, which sank beneath the waves.

Míriel tried to reach the sacred peak of Meneltarma in the centre of Númenor, but she was swept from the side of the mountain by the great wave, victim and pawn in a game played by men of vain pride and foolishness.

— The Silmarillion, 'Akallabêth'

ROHAN's King Théoden survived many battles in his life, leading countless charges upon his faithful steed, Snowmane. But in the decisive Battle of the Pelennor Fields outside the city of Minas Tirith, not even Snowmane could withstand the fury and fear instilled by the Witch-king of Angmar upon his fell beast. Snowmane, terrified of the approaching flying beast, panicked and Théoden was mortally wounded when the horse fell upon him.

He was avenged soon after, however, as the Hobbit Merry plunged his Barrow-blade into the Witch-king's leg, the power of that blade breaking the spell of invulnerability around him. The lady Éowyn, hitherto disguised as a Rider of Rohan named Dernhelm, then revealed herself and thrust her blade into the Lord of the Nazgûl's head, killing him. Théoden was eventually interred in Edoras with great honour, and his nephew Éomer succeeded him as King of Rohan.

— The Return of the King, 'The Battle of the Pelennor Fields'

SARUMAN the White, one of the first of the Istari to arrive in Middle-earth, was head of the White Council, and for many years a trusted and wise counsellor. He eventually fell victim to his wizard's own hubris and ambition when the Ents defeated him and took Isengard. Even though his wizard's staff was broken by Gandalf and with his power seemingly gone, Saruman managed to slip away and wreak havoc in the Shire under the guise of a petty criminal lord called Sharkey.

In the end, Saruman pushed his servant/slave Wormtongue too far, and in his rage, Wormtongue cut Saruman's throat. Saruman's human form lost its shape, but being a Maia his spirit could not be killed. Because of his ambition and betrayal, Saruman's spirit was forbidden from returning to the West, and he was doomed to wander Middle-earth unable to ever find rest.

— *The Return of the King*, 'The Scouring of the Shire'

TÚRIN TURAMBAR's tale is akin to a high Greek tragedy, with twists and turns, and terrible secrets and revelations.

He is a victim of both a curse laid upon his family tree, and of his own actions and pride, which exacerbate the terrible events. When he seemed to have found peace and thought that the curse was over, he called himself 'Turambar', which means 'Master of Fate'. That is never a smart idea, and the mighty Dragon Glaurung, who had deceived him in the past, pursued him to where Túrin abode. With his black-bladed sword, Gurthang, he managed to slay the Dragon. But the curse would not be so easily denied, and with his dying breath, Glaurung revealed a terrible truth to Túrin. Túrin's spirit finally broke, and he impaled himself upon the blackness of Gurthang.

— The Children of Húrin

UNGOLIANT is a malevolent spirit-being in the form of a monstrous spider, destroyer of the Two Trees, and ally and foe of Morgoth. She came from the darkness that lay outside of Arda and existed before existence itself. She was the only creature who worked with Morgoth, and not for him. He feared her insatiable lust for and hatred of light, and after they had killed the Two Trees and stolen the Silmarils, she grew monstrously huge from what she had consumed and trapped Morgoth in her web. His cries for help shook the very mountains, and he only escaped because a large group of Balrogs came to save him.

Ungoliant fled south to Beleriand, and there hid deep in darkness, mating with other foul creatures, and devouring them as well. The mighty spider Shelob was one of her children, as were the spiders of Mirkwood. It is said that in the end, her insatiable hunger drove her to consume herself, bringing to an end one of the most powerful and terrifying creations in all of Tolkien's works.

— The Silmarillion, 'Of the Flight of the Noldor'

VALIANT ORI was one of the thirteen Dwarves who set out to reclaim their homeland of Erebor from Smaug. He was the cousin of Dori and Nori, and fought with great honour in the Battle of the Five Armies. He received his share of the treasure and settled down in Erebor.

Somewhere around fifty years after the adventure with Bilbo and the Dragon, a group of Dwarves led by Balin decided to return to Khazad-dûm, or Moria as it was also known. Moria had been lost to the Dwarves around a thousand years earlier when Durin VI's people delved too deep seeking *mithril* and unleashed the Balrog that would later kill Gandalf the Grey.

Balin hoped to reclaim Moria, but though his expedition had initially found some success, within five years the Orcs of Moria had killed all of the Dwarves who returned. Balin was laid to rest in the Chamber of Mazarbul, and that was where the last stand of the remaining Dwarves took place.

Ori had been keeping a record of their time in Khazad-dûm, and he bravely continued to write right up until the very end when he was slain by the Orcs. The last line of the Book of Mazarbul being: 'They are coming.'

— *The Fellowship of the Ring*, 'The Bridge of Khazad-dûm'

The **WITCH-KING OF ANGMAR**, Lord of the Nazgûl, Chief of Sauron's lieutenants, has a story that spans over 4,000 years. His origins, like all of the Nazgûl, are shrouded in mystery, but he was likely one of three Númenórean lords, and a powerful sorcerer, who accepted one of the 'Nine Rings for Mortal Men Doomed to Die' from Sauron; and it gave him great power.

But of course, it also bound him in servitude to the Dark Lord, and when his mortal body died, his spirit lived on as a wraith. He led many armies in battle against Elves and Men, and the Elf-Lord Glorfindel prophesied 'Far off yet is his doom, and not by the hand of man will he fall.'

And so it would prove. When the soldier of Rohan named Dernhelm defended the body of the fallen King Théoden, the Witch-king gloated 'Thou fool! No living man may hinder me!' Then Dernhelm removed his helmet, revealing he was, in fact, the shieldmaiden of Rohan, Éowyn. Merry the Hobbit, also in the battle as an esquire of Rohan, then drew out the Barrow-blade he obtained earlier in the story from the Barrow-wights. Being made long ago by the Dúnedain in the war against Angmar, it pierced the back of the leg of the Witch-king, and broke the spell of invulnerability that protected him. Despite her shattered arm and wounds received from the Lord of the Nazgûl, Éowyn was able to thrust her sword into his head, destroying him.

— The Return of the King, 'The Battle of the Pelennor Fields'

X – GIMLI'S AXE. One of the delights of reading *The Lord of the Rings* is the friendship between Legolas and Gimli that evolves over the story and far into the Appendices. A stand-out moment in the books and the movies is their contest to see who can slay more Orcs at Helm's Deep. There's something about their bravado and increasing respect and care for one another.

'He had no helm, and about his head was a linen band stained with blood; but his voice was loud and strong.

'Forty-two, Master Legolas!' he cried. 'Alas! My axe is notched: the forty-second had an iron collar on his neck. How is it with you?'

'You have passed my score by one,' answered Legolas. 'But I do not grudge you the game, so glad am I to see you on your legs!'

— *The Two Towers*, 'The Road to Isengard'

YOUNG THÉODRED, the only son of King Théoden of Rohan, died at the Fords of Isen, ambushed by an army of Orcs sent by Saruman. This was all part of Saruman's plan to weaken Rohan to prove to Sauron his loyalty, even as he plotted to find the One Ring for himself. In the book, Théodred is buried in a hastily created mound on a small area of land in the Fords of Isen, but I chose the powerful moment from the film where Théoden buries his son outside of Edoras.

Théodred is actually forty-one when he dies, so the term 'youthful' might be stretching it a bit. However, as a parent, I'm sure King Théoden would forever consider Théodred his little boy, forever young. The movie *The Two Towers* came out in 2002, and the scene where the late, great Bernard Hill delivers the line 'No parent should ever bury their child' was heart wrenching. My first child was born in 2005, and I remember watching that scene again after that, and I had to pause the film because of the tears streaming down my face. Forever young, indeed.

— *Unfinished Tales*, 'The Battles of the Fords of Isen'

ZIRAKZIGIL, one of three great mountain peaks above Khazad-dûm, is where Gandalf and the Balrog known as Durin's Bane ended their battle after ten days and nights of fighting. Gandalf was finally able to slay the great demon of Morgoth and threw down his enemy on the mountainside where he smote it in his ruin. This all happened near the ruins of Durin's Tower and the Endless Stair that rose from the depths of the Mines of Moria to the summit of Zirakzigil (known also as Celebdil). Gandalf's spirit left his body, but Eru Ilúvatar sent him back to complete his mission, more powerful than ever as Gandalf the White.

This is one of the pivotal moments in *The Lord of the Rings*. Gandalf was now considered to be the only one of the original five Istari (Wizards) to stay true to his original purpose, and was now allowed to use more of his power as a Maia.

Later, he and Aragorn would lead the army of the West to the Black Gates of Mordor, where Gandalf would chastise and dismiss the mighty Mouth of Sauron, and fight the massive armies of Mordor, buying time for Frodo and Sam to destroy the Ring (with Gollum's "help").

It is upon the peak of Zirakzigil where the tide would turn, and Gandalf the Grey would become Gandalf the White, and change the fate of the world.

— *The Two Towers*, 'The White Rider'

ACKNOWLEDGEMENTS

Working out who to thank for the book that you are holding is possibly the scariest thing I have ever done. So many people have shaped me in one way or another that I must I beg forgiveness of anyone I have left off this list!

It is always best to start with a strong foundation, and for almost 35 years, that has been my wife, Kim Hendrix. That foundation was made even stronger in 2005 and 2008 by my children Katie and Sam. All three are my heart, my inspiration, and my love. I am so proud of them, the art and music they create in their own lives, and without them, none of this happens.

Going back further, two of my brothers were especially influential in my artistic life. Don and Bill, sadly both recipients of the Gift of Ilúvatar, encouraged their annoying little brother by introducing me to comic books, science fiction (*Star Trek* and *Star Wars*), *Dungeons & Dragons*, and J.R.R. Tolkien. In 1977 when I was eleven years old, two major events happened; *Star Wars* came out, and *The Silmarillion* was published. For Christmas, Don and Bill got me *The Star Wars Sketchbook*, which introduced the idea into my brain that artists could get paid to draw fun stuff, and the 1978 *The Lord of the Rings Calendar*, illustrated by the Brothers Hildebrandt. Over the years, Don and Bill would share their love of reading and movies with me, always encouraging me to work on my art. They set me on this path, and it pains me that I can't hand them copies of this book and thank them with all my heart. But, in the words of Théoden King, 'Hail the Victorious Dead!'

In a very real sense, this book only exists because it was championed by David Brawn at HarperCollins. His enthusiasm and support of my work has truly been a high point in my professional artistic career, and banished all my imposter-syndrome demons to the darkness from which they were spawned. I thank him and the team around him who shaped what I sent them into this gorgeous little book.

My cartoonist/writer friends have been there with support, words of advice, and deep friendship over many years: Lucas Turnbloom, Justin Thompson, Lincoln Peirce, Francesco Marciuliano, Terri Libenson, Maria Scrivan, and many other cartoonist and writing colleagues I have known through comic conventions, meet ups, and podcasts.

It was the response of people on Instagram, especially of the Tolkien friends I have made on there, that sparked the dream of turning my Inktober 2024 posts into a book in the first place. So many of these amazing Tolkien-inspired creators have in turn inspired me in ways I can't articulate. The list of people I interact with and have befriended grows all the time, and I thank everyone who has shared my work, encouraged me, and given me such love and confidence to grow as an artist. You lit the Beacons of Gondor down a path I never considered, and helped me take my first steps down it.

Finally, of course, I acknowledge two of the great artistic inspirations of my entire life. Professor John Ronald Reuel Tolkien, and Edward Gorey. I have spent so many hours of my life exploring both your worlds, and it is beyond my wildest dreams that this book, an homage from the heart to both of you, exists. Thank you for all the adventure and joy.

TOM RACINE
June 2025